A REAL LIVE PET!

by Lydia Lukidis

illustrated by Craig Cameron

Kane Press
New York

For my beautiful daughter Emerald Skye, who lights up my world and continues to inspire me every day—L.L.

For Ellie, Lewis & Joe—C.C.

Acknowledgements: Our thanks to Rebeka Eston Salemi, Kindergarten Teacher, Lincoln School, Lincoln, MA, for helping us make this book as accurate as possible. Special thanks to Meagan Branday Susi for providing the activities in the back of this book.

Library of Congress Cataloging-in-Publication Data
Names: Lukidis, Lydia, author. | Cameron, Craig, illustrator.
Title: A real live pet! / by Lydia Lukidis ; illustrated by Craig Cameron.
Description: New York : Kane Press, 2018. | Series: Science solves it! |
    Summary: Told he cannot have a pet for his birthday, JJ catches a frog and
    his sister, Nala, finds a pet branch, which leads to a lesson about living
    and nonliving things. Includes an activity sheet.
Identifiers: LCCN 2017038098 (print) | LCCN 2017022516 (ebook) | ISBN
    9781635920109 () | ISBN 9781635920093 (pbk. : alk. paper)
Subjects: | CYAC: Pets--Fiction. | Natural science--Fiction. |
    Birthdays--Fiction. | Family life--Fiction.
Classification: LCC PZ7.1.L845 (print) | LCC PZ7.1.L845 Re 2018 (ebook) | DDC
    [E]--dc23
LC record available at https://lccn.loc.gov/2017038098

10 9 8 7 6 5 4 3 2 1

First published in the United States of America in 2018 by Kane Press, Inc.
Printed in China

Science Solves It! is a registered trademark of Kane Press, Inc.

Book Design: Michelle Martinez

Visit us online at **www.kanepress.com**

 Like us on Facebook
facebook.com/kanepress

 Follow us on Twitter
@KanePress

"Only TWO more sleeps until my birthday!"
sang JJ. He hopped around the kitchen.

JJ had been begging his parents for a pet.
"So what are you going to get me?" he asked
them. "A tarantula? A lizard? Or maybe a—"

"Now Jelani," Mom said with a serious face. "I told you pets are too much work."

JJ sighed and plopped into a chair.

"Cheer up," Mom went on. "We're going to the nature center tomorrow. They have plenty of animals there for you to *look at*."

"I have an idea," JJ whispered to his sister, Nala, after breakfast. "I'm going to find a pet myself!"

He grabbed his net and bucket. Nala's eyes widened.

"Me too," she squealed. "I want a pet, too!"

They told their parents they were going to play near the pond by their house. When they got there, JJ looked around. It was quiet, until—

RIBBIT, RIBBIT!

"Aha!" he said. "Listen to that!"

JJ followed the croaking sound. Then he spotted the most awesome frog. It was big and green and spotty.

He got his net ready and threw it over the frog. *Victory!*

"He's a whopper!" Nala said.

"Thanks!" JJ said, beaming. Then he looked at his sister. "What are you doing?"

Nala was hugging a huge oak tree. "This is my pet," she said.

JJ laughed. "A tree? It can't fit in our house!"

Nala frowned for a moment. Then she picked up a branch.

"My pet," she said proudly. She cradled the branch in her arms like a baby.

JJ shook his head. But he didn't have time to argue. He wanted to rush home to show off his frog.

"You'll never guess what I caught," he said as he ran inside. "A real live FROG!"

Dad smiled. But Mom didn't look too pleased.

Nala also showed off her branch.

"A branch can't be a pet," JJ said. "It's not even alive. It doesn't have a face!"

"Well," Dad said, "living things don't always have faces. Look at trees or flowers."

JJ sighed. Dad loved science. And he *really* loved talking about science.

"But that branch was just lying dead on the ground," JJ pointed out.

"Ah, that's where the science gets tricky," said Dad. "The branch may be dead now, but it's still a *living thing*. That's different from a *nonliving thing*."

A living thing is either alive or was once alive, like a dog, a seed, or a flower—even if the flower has been cut.

JJ scrunched up his face. "So what's a nonliving thing?"

"It's something that is not alive and never was," Dad said. "Like a rock. Or a car. Get it?"

"I guess so," JJ said slowly. "But I still don't think a branch can be a pet."

A nonliving thing is not alive and never was, like something made out of stone or plastic.

"I think a branch is a very creative pet," Mom said. "Nala, you can keep it." Then Mom turned to JJ. "As for that frog . . . I'm afraid you'll have to return it to the pond."

"Please," JJ begged, "can't I keep him for just one day? I could take him to the nature center tomorrow. They could teach me about frogs and living things and everything! Right, Dad?"

Dad grinned but said, "It's up to your mother."
Even Nala put on her best pleading look.
Mom sighed. "Fine. *One* day. But find somewhere
to keep him so he doesn't hop all over the house!"

Sweet! JJ found a plastic container and poked holes through the lid. Nala put in a handful of leaves. "To make him cozy!" she said.

JJ gently placed the frog in the container. Nala giggled. "He sure likes to hop around!"

"That's it!" JJ said. "I'll call him Hopper."

People, animals, insects, trees, grass, and other plants are all examples of living things.

The next day, they went to the nature center. JJ's favorite room had lots of reptiles in glass tanks. He spotted a big snake.

"That snake is huge," he said to Nala.

"Sure is!" a friendly voice behind them said. It was a nature center guide.

"My name's Darlene," she told them. "And that there is a python. Pythons are some of the longest snakes in the world!"

"That's cool," said JJ. "But I have an even cooler animal."

He opened his container to show off Hopper.

"Gadzooks!" Darlene said. "That sure is neat. That's a *Rana catesbeiana*! Also known as a good old American bullfrog."

"I have a pet, too!" Nala said. She held out her branch. "This is Sparky!"

JJ rolled his eyes. "I still say a branch isn't a real pet."

Darlene laughed. "Why not?"

"Pets should be alive," JJ said. "And I'm not talking about *living things*. I mean a pet should, you know, move!"

"Actually, plenty of living things don't move much, but they're still alive. Like mushrooms," said Darlene. "And some things move around, but they're not alive at all. Like water. Weird, huh?"

"For sure." JJ nodded.

Some nonliving things move but are not alive, like fire and water.

"Now get this," Darlene went on. "All living things eat, breathe, reproduce, grow, move, and give off waste. That means they poop!"

JJ laughed. "Hopper definitely poops!"

Nala frowned. "Sparky definitely doesn't."

"Well, let me explain," Darlene told her. "Animals get rid of waste in their bodies by pooping. Plants get rid of waste by giving off gases. It's just a different way of doing the same thing!"

Nala looked hopeful. "So my branch can be a pet?"

Darlene smiled. "Almost anything can be a pet! When I was your age, I had a pet named Hubert."

"What kind of animal was Hubert?" JJ asked.

Darlene burst out laughing. "He was a pet rock!"

Nonliving things come in three groups: solids, liquids, and gases. Water is a liquid. It is not alive. Oxygen is a gas. It is not alive. A rock is a solid. It is not alive.

Nala loved the idea of a pet rock. She said she wanted one, too! But JJ still thought Hopper was cooler. He looked down to admire the frog. But the lid of the container was open.

"CODE RED!" he shrieked. "Hopper is gone!"

JJ ran around in a panic. He looked in
the animal displays. He checked the plants.
He searched all the tanks. Nala and Darlene
pitched in, too.

But Hopper was nowhere to be seen.

JJ slumped down on a bench. He knew
Hopper wasn't really his pet. But what if he
was gone forever?

RIBBIT, RIBBIT!

Something slimy jumped right onto JJ's foot. "HOPPER! You came back!"

JJ picked up the frog and held it gently. His birthday wasn't until tomorrow, but he made a wish anyway. He wished to never lose Hopper again.

When they got home later, JJ grabbed his net and flashlight. "Time for dinner, Hopper."

He trapped a few moths, just like Darlene had taught him. Then he fed them to Hopper.

"JJ," Nala said, "do you still want a new pet for your birthday?"

"I did want a tarantula," JJ said. "But now . . ."
He sniffled quietly. He knew he would have
to say goodbye to Hopper soon.

Mom came to the back door. "Why don't
you keep that frog one more night, JJ?" she
said. "After all, it's your birthday tomorrow."

JJ smiled. "Thanks, Mom."

The next morning, JJ's family was waiting for him downstairs. A big present sat on the table. JJ ripped off the paper. It was a glass tank! But there was no pet inside it. JJ was confused.

Mom beamed. "It's a proper home for Hopper!" she said. "Dad and I saw how well you took care of him."

HAPPY BIRTHDAY JJ

"You mean I can keep him?" asked JJ.
His parents nodded.

"Thank you, thank you, thank you!" JJ said.
He pranced around the kitchen. Then he placed
his pet frog in its new home. Hopper hopped
around happily.

Nala also had a gift for her brother. She handed him a little rock. She had painted it green. There were googly eyes on it.

"It's a pet rock for Hopper," she said. "Her name is Sparky Junior."

JJ gave Nala a big hug. "Thanks, Nala," he said. "I'm sorry I made fun of your branch. And you know what? I'm pretty sure that between Hopper and Sparky, you and I have the greatest pets in the world."

THINK LIKE A SCIENTIST

JJ and Nala think like scientists—and so can you!

Living things all eat, breathe, reproduce, grow, move, and give off waste. Plants do these things differently than humans. They "eat" by taking in nutrition from the soil. They "move" by turning their leaves toward the sun.

JJ learned that Nala's branch was a living thing because it was once part of a tree. You can think like a scientist and compare living and nonliving things around you if you know what to look for!

Look Back

- Look back at page 15. Why did JJ poke holes in the container?
- Re-read what Darlene says about living things on pages 19–20. Brainstorm a list of living things.

Try This!

Paint Your Own Pet Rock

Nala made a pet rock-frog as a birthday present for JJ. To make your own pet rock, you will need: a rock, paint, a paintbrush, a cup of water, and a pencil or chalk.

Use a pencil or piece of chalk to draw your favorite animal on the rock. Then paint it in.

Give your pet a name and find a nice home for it. And remember—the best part of having a pet rock is that nonliving things can't get into any trouble!